The Way to
Wyatt's House

The Way to Wyatt's House

Nancy White Carlstrom

Illustrations by **Mary Morgan**

Walker & Company
NEW YORK

For my nephew, Wyatt Lawrence Brown, with love.
—N. W. C.

To my mother and father.
—M. M.

please come over and play! Wyatt

Text copyright © 2000 by Nancy White Carlstrom
Illustrations copyright © 2000 by Mary Morgan

First published in the United States of America in 2000 by Walker Publishing Company, Inc.
Published simultaneously in Canada by Fitzhenry and Whiteside, Markham, Ontario L3R 4T8

Library of Congress Cataloging–in–Publication Data

Carlstrom, Nancy White.
    The way to Wyatt's house / Nancy White Carlstrom ; illustrations by Mary Morgan.
      p. cm.
    Summary: Two children have fun visiting their friend Wyatt's farm.
    ISBN 0–8027–8740–1 — ISBN 0–8027–8742–8 (reinforced)
    [1. Friendship—Fiction. 2. Farms—Fiction. 3. Domestic animals—Fiction.]
    I. Morgan-Vanroyen, Mary, 1957– ill. II. Title.

PZ7.C21684 Way 2000   00–028999
[E]—dc21

Book design by Rosanne Kakos-Main

Printed in Hong Kong
10 9 8 7 6 5 4 3 2

This is the quiet way
we walk to Wyatt's house.
We tiptoe out, silent as shy mice,
and let the door sigh shut.

AAH AAH AAH!

We follow the path through the trees
where the leaves float down.
They curl on beds of brown hard ground.

We leave our footprints behind
making a thin crunching sound.

CRINCH CRINCH CRINCH!

The breeze blows the thick fuzz
off the sticky bushes.

FOOSH FOOSH FOOSH

Don't let it tickle your nose.
It will make you sneeze.

BLESS YOU! BLESS YOU!

This is the quiet way we walk to Wyatt's house.
We climb over fallen logs, as if they are mountains.

And we bend to see the little beetles
who scurry into the ground.

CLICK
CLICK
CLICK
CLICK

When we reach the meadow with the long grass
we are almost there.
Even the grass whispers

SWOOSH SWOOSH SWOOSH

on the swishing way to Wyatt's house.

And now we see Wyatt watching us from the window.

WE ARE HERE!
WE ARE HERE!

We yell
as we jump out of quiet into

LOUD!

Wyatt, our best friend,
comes running, **SCREAMING**

twirling, whirling
down the hill to greet us.

HOORAY!
HOORAY!

He yells in his hardly-ever-quiet
Wyatt voice.

FINALLY YOU ARE HERE!

This is the way we are welcomed to Wyatt's house.

Iris and Buttercup dance out to meet us
on their little tapping goat feet.
They sing **maa maa maa**
as they prance up the hill behind us.

Jack the Cat pounces
out of the shadows and announces
in his great Black Jack meowing voice:
meow meow meow.

WOOF
WOOF
SLURP SLURP!

Phoebe the dog barks and barks
and licks and licks.

Phoebe knows very little about quiet ways,
but she knows a lot about love.

The chickens rush out of their coop
pecking and clucking
and chucking their words
into the crisp autumn air.

CHICKA

CHICKA

Old Rooster decides to crow
for the second time that day.

COCK–A–DOODLE

QUACK
ACK
ACK

Ducks waddle their way up from the pond
in whole families.
All the noisy afternoon
we play at Wyatt's house.

QUACK
ACK
ACK

We have not run out of noise or games to play
when we hear the **toot toot** of Daddy's car horn.
It is time to go home, our mama says.

Wyatt's loud, loud

GOOD–BYE

follows us
down the long, twisting road,
and before we know it
we are leaving loud
drifting into quiet
going
the sleepy way home.

SSHH SSHH SSHH